The
a

FREE THE
GALAXY

Written by Himani Khatreja

Editor Himani Khatreja
Art Editor Nathan Martin
Editorial Assistant Rosie Peet
Assistant Art Editor Akansha Jain
DTP Designers Umesh Singh Rawat, Rajdeep Singh
Pre-Production Producer Marc Staples
Pre-Production Manager Sunil Sharma
Producer Louise Daly
Managing Editors Simon Hugo, Chitra Subramanyam
Managing Art Editors Neha Ahuja, Guy Harvey
Art Director Lisa Lanzarini
Publisher Julie Ferris
Publishing Director Simon Beecroft

Reading Consultant Maureen Fernandes

Dorling Kindersley would like to thank
Randi Sørensen, Paul Hansford and Robert Stefan Ekblom
at the LEGO Group.

For Lucasfilm
Executive Editor Jonathan W. Rinzler
Art Director Troy Alders
Story Group Rayne Roberts, Pablo Hidalgo, Leland Chee

First published in 2015 in Great Britain by Dorling Kindersley Limited
80 Strand, London, WC2R 0RL
A Penguin Random House Company

10 9 8 7 6 5 4 3 2 1
001–279703–September/2015

A CIP catalogue record for this book is available from the British Library.

ISBN: 978-0-24118-682-4

Printed in China

www.LEGO.com
www.starwars.com
www.dk.com

A WORLD OF IDEAS:
SEE ALL THERE IS TO KNOW

Contents

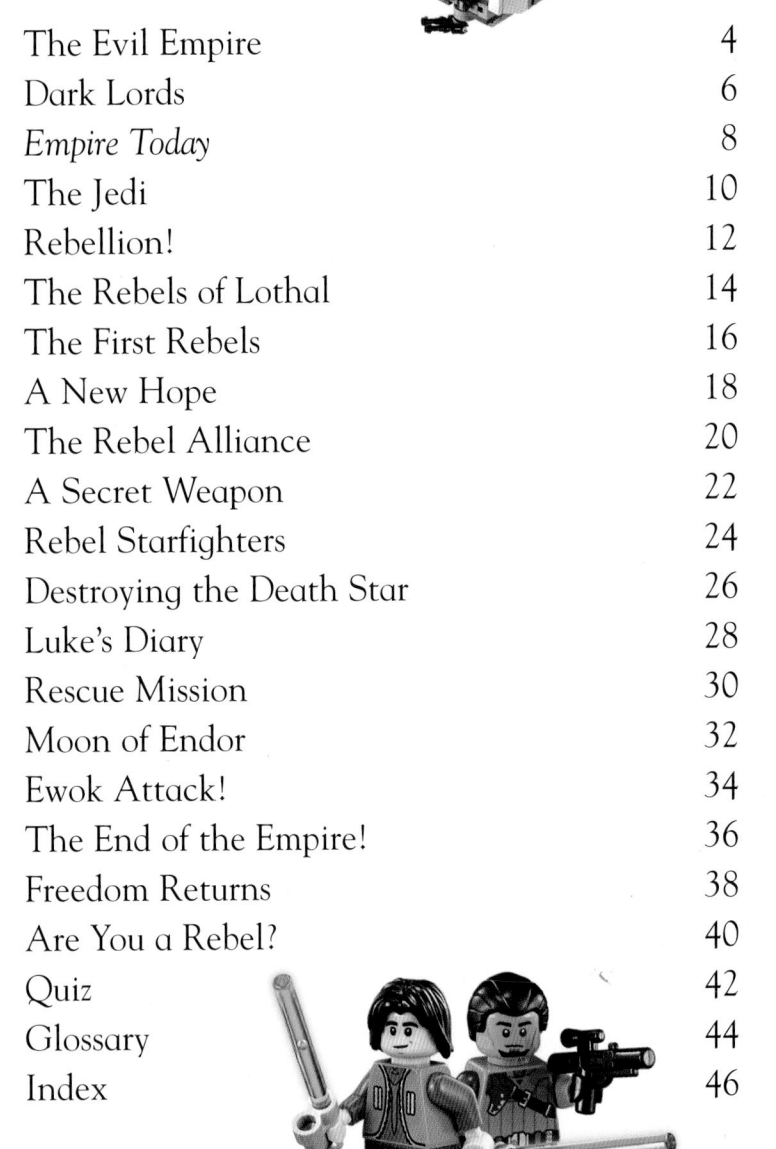

The Evil Empire

An evil Empire has taken
over the galaxy.
It is using its mighty army
and powerful starships
to bully helpless citizens.

Anyone who dares to speak up is punished. Is there anyone out there brave enough to stand up to the Empire and free the galaxy?

Dark Lords

Just hearing the names of
Emperor Palpatine and
his apprentice, Darth Vader,
can make people tremble.
These Dark Lords have
taken charge of the galaxy.
They love rules and making
life hard for anyone who
breaks them.

EMPIRE

Volume IX

The Empire Turns 14.
Celebrate or else!

The Emperor looks radiant in his trademark black.

TODAY

By *Empire Today* Reporter

It was 14 years ago today that the supremely intelligent and handsome Emperor Palpatine took over the galaxy. He has ordered all citizens to celebrate Empire Day and say nice things about the Empire – or else. Speaking on the occasion, the Emperor said, "Each of you insignificant mortals is lucky to have a ruler like me. Now go away!"

"I will destroy anyone who dares to rebel against the great Emperor."

– Darth Vader

"The Emperor is our leader. Errm, he is always right. Usually..."

– Brave stormtrooper

The Jedi

Once, the Jedi warriors were
protectors of peace and justice.
They used a mysterious
power called the Force to
defend those in peril.
But nearly all of the Jedi
were destroyed by the Empire.
Who will defend the
galaxy now?

Rebellion!

People are rising up all
across the galaxy to rebel
against the Empire.
They want to be free.

They want to bring back peace
and happiness to the galaxy.
These rebels are determined
to fight for a better future, no
matter how long it takes!

The Rebels of Lothal

On the planet Lothal, a small group of feisty rebels is fighting to make life hard for the Empire.

They enjoy blowing up starships
and fooling stormtroopers.
These rebels know it will be
a long fight, but one day they
hope the galaxy will be free.

THE FIRST REBELS

The Empire has done everything it can to destroy the rebels of Lothal. But the six rebels always manage to escape the Imperial officers!

KANAN

Jedi and rebel leader

Good at: Planning missions and using the Force

Weapons: Lightsaber and a blaster

Rebel tactic: Using his lightsaber lightning-fast

EZRA

Jedi-in-training

Good at: Crawling through tiny spaces

Weapon: Lightsaber that is also a blaster

Rebel tactic: Being sneaky and running really, really fast

SABINE

Explosives expert and artist

Good at: Making explosives

Weapons: Twin blasters and explosives

Rebel tactic: Blowing up the Empire's property

Ace pilot and Captain of the *Ghost*

Good at: Keeping the team together

Weapon: Blaster

Rebel tactic: Flying the rebels out of tricky situations

HERA

ZEB

Highly trained Lasat warrior

Good at: Hand-to-hand combat

Weapon: Bo-rifle

Rebel tactic: Being stronger than everyone else

Astromech droid

Good at: Fixing the *Ghost* and keeping it running

Weapon: Booster rocket

Rebel tactic: Distracting the Empire's soldiers and zapping droids

CHOPPER

A New Hope!

The rebels have fought
the Empire for years.
They have caused lots of
trouble for the Empire, but have
still not managed to destroy it.
Now a Rebel Alliance has
been formed. It has a special
member called Luke Skywalker.
This brave young man may
finally be able to defeat
the Emperor.

THE REBEL ALLIANCE

LUKE SKYWALKER
Farm boy and Jedi

Expert at flying the
X-wing starfighter

Can't wait to use the Force
to help his friends

EMPIRE BEWARE
Luke is great
at blowing up
Imperial
starfighters.

EMPIRE BEWARE
Leia is good
at stealing
secret plans.

LEIA ORGANA
Senior rebel leader and princess

Knows exactly how to beat
up stormtroopers

Thinks Han is handsome, but
very rude and not at all funny

The Empire had better be scared of the Rebel Alliance. So what if its members include a farm boy, a smuggler, a princess and a Wookiee? Together, they are unbeatable!

HAN SOLO
Smuggler and captain of the *Millennium Falcon*

Leads missions against the Empire and wins... mostly

Thinks he is very handsome and extremely funny

EMPIRE BEWARE
Han can escape Imperial starfighters in the Falcon.

EMPIRE BEWARE
Stormtroopers should avoid being around when Chewie loses his temper.

CHEWBACCA
Wookiee warrior and co-pilot of the *Millennium Falcon*

Will do anything for friends, even fight stormtroopers

Likes Jedi and fixing broken droids

A Secret Weapon

The rebels have really been making Darth Vader sweat. Now Vader is ready to fight back with the Death Star. It is a weapon so deadly that it can destroy entire planets! What Darth Vader doesn't know yet is that a clever rebel called Princess Leia has stolen the plans for how the Death Star works.

REBEL
STARFIGHTERS

These mighty starfighters are ready for battle, whether on the icy-cold planet of Hoth, or over the jungles of Yavin 4. The rebels are ready to fly!

X-wing

Astromech droid

Pilot cockpit

Engine

- Easily dodges Empire's zippy fighters
- Wings fold into attack mode
- Small enough to fly into the Death Star's trenches

A-wing

The high-speed A-wing is perfect for quick attacks.

One of four wings

Laser gun

B-wing

The B-wing is loaded with missiles and weapons.

Destroying the Death Star

The rebels use the Death Star's
plans to find its weak spot.
This is the X-wing
pilots' only chance.
Their best pilot, Luke
Skywalker, flies his X-wing
at the Death Star.
He blows it to pieces
in a single shot!

Luke's Diary

Day 48

After we blew up the Death Star, Darth Vader was so angry that we decided the best thing would be to hide. So we built this base on Hoth. Boy, it is cold!

I had to do some quick Jedi tricks to escape the hungry wampa!

Day 51

Yesterday, I stuck my tongue out and it turned into an icicle! A few days before that, I was out on my tauntaun and got kidnapped by this scary wampa creature. I'm not crazy about Hoth.

Leia, Han and I had a clever plan to deal with these AT-ATs.

Day 55

Today, the Empire found us! The AT-ATs were headed our way and we had to distract them. We flew our snowspeeders around the AT-ATs, wrapping cables around their legs. Some of them toppled over. We escaped while they were untangling themselves. Take that, Darth Vader!

Rescue Mission

The Empire has
captured Han Solo.
Darth Vader has frozen
him in carbonite.
Han is not very happy.
He is alive, but trapped!
The rebels don't abandon
their friends, so Lando and
Leia disguise themselves
and stage a daring rescue.
Han knew he could count
on his friends!

MOON OF ENDOR

A REPORT FOR
The Evil Empire

GOAL: To find out if the forest moon of Endor is a good place to put the shield generator for the Empire's new Death Star.

ORDERED BY:
Emperor Palpatine

LOCATION: Far away in an unexplored part of the galaxy. Close to the Death Star.

WEATHER: Mild. Not too hot or cold. A very cool breeze, too.

POPULATION: Mainly short, furry creatures called Ewoks. Do not cuddle them. They bite.

LAND: Thick green forest made up of very, very tall trees. Be careful while riding speeder bikes.

RESULT:
Endor is the perfect place! The tall trees will keep the shield generator hidden. It will be safe from the rebels, who will never be able to find it. The Ewoks use spears. They are no match for the Empire's blasters.

APPROVED

Ewok Attack!

The rebels are under attack from stormtroopers on Endor. The Ewoks, who live there, decide to help the rebels.

They launch sticks and stones to distract the stormtroopers. With the stormtroopers off their guard, the rebels can attack. They destroy the shield generator that protects the new Death Star.

Luke has found out that Darth Vader is his father! Now the Emperor is making them fight. Could this finally be...

THE END OF THE EMPIRE!

2 The fight begins. Vader is surprised by Luke's skill.

4 Vader does not want to see his son destroyed, so he turns against the Emperor to protect Luke.

Freedom Returns

The Empire has been defeated,
thanks to each and every
rebel's heroic efforts.
The rebels can now celebrate,
as fireworks light up the sky.

Our heroes will face more
challenges in the future.
The dark side is
never far away.
But for now, all is well
and the galaxy is free.

ARE YOU A REBEL?

Emperor Palpatine was very powerful, but he only cared about himself. The rebels fought for freedom and to protect others. What would you do? Which side are you on?

START HERE

Do you like being part of a team?

YES

Is winning more important than your friends?

NO

YES

Do you only care about yourself?

YES

Do you tell lies to get what you want?

NO

YES

Do you like blue or green lightsabers?

NO

YES

NO → Is it nice to help people? → YES

NO

Do you like being angry?

NO → NO

YES

YOU ARE NOT A REBEL. JOIN THE EMPIRE.

YOU ARE A REBEL. JOIN THE REBEL ALLIANCE.

4

Quiz

1. Who are the two dark lords who have taken over the galaxy?

2. On Empire Day, how long had the Empire ruled the galaxy?

3. What special power do the Jedi use?

4. Which rebel of Lothal uses a bo-rifle as his weapon?

5. Who is the Rebel Alliance's special member?

6. Who steals the plans to the Death Star?

7. Which team of pilots help Luke destroy the first Death Star?

8. Which furry creature kidnaps Luke on Hoth?

9. Where do the Ewoks live?

10. Who is Luke Skywalker's father?

Answers on page 47

Glossary

Alliance
An agreement between people who share the same goal

Apprentice
A person who is learning a skill

Citizen
A person who lives in a city or town

Droid
A type of robot

Heroic
Brave

Imperial
Relating to the Empire

Insignificant
Not important

Peril
Serious danger

Radiant
Looking bright and happy

Smuggler
Someone who transports things
secretly so they can make money
from selling them

Starship
A vehicle used for travel
between stars

Answers to the quiz on pages 42 and 43:
1. Emperor Palpatine and Darth Vader
2. 14 years 3. The Force 4. Zeb 5. Luke Skywalker
6. Princess Leia 7. X-wing pilots 8. Wampa creature
9. Moon of Endor 10. Darth Vader

Index

Have you read these other great books from DK?

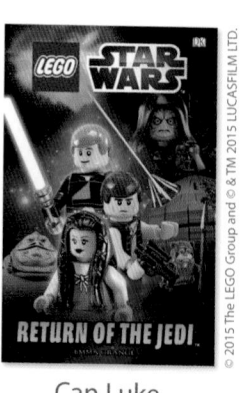

Join Luke Skywalker and his friends on their adventures.

Can the rebels survive the brutal assault of the Imperial forces?

Can Luke Skywalker help the rebels defeat the evil Empire?

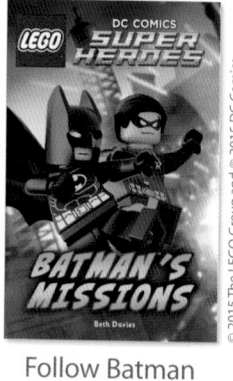

Who has brought the galaxy to the brink of war? Can the Jedi stop them?

There are villains on the rampage! Who will keep the world safe?

Follow Batman as he fights to protect Gotham City from crime.